OCT			
			PRINTED IN U.S.A.

by Jenna Lynn   illustrated by Abigail Dela Cruz

ROBYN HOOD

METROPOLIS ORPHANAGE

Spellbound

An Imprint of Magic Wagon
abdobooks.com

To my family, who have been my strongest supporters,
Dad, Mom, Zandra, Berna, Wowo, Mama and Tita Beth —ADC

For my family —JL

abdobooks.com

Published by Magic Wagon, a division of ABDO, PO Box 398166, Minneapolis,
Minnesota 55439. Copyright © 2019 by Abdo Consulting Group, Inc. International
copyrights reserved in all countries. No part of this book may be reproduced in any
form without written permission from the publisher. Spellbound™ is a trademark and
logo of Magic Wagon.

Printed in the United States of America, North Mankato, Minnesota.
092018
012019

THIS BOOK CONTAINS
RECYCLED MATERIALS

Written by Jenna Lynn
Illustrated by Abigail Dela Cruz
Edited by Bridget O'Brien
Design Contributors: Victoria Bates, Candice Keimig and Laura Mitchell

Library of Congress Control Number: 2018947815

Publisher's Cataloging-in-Publication Data

Names: Lynn, Jenna, author. | Dela Cruz, Abigail, illustrator.
Title: Metropolis Orphanage / by Jenna Lynn; illustrated by Abigail Dela Cruz.
Description: Minneapolis, Minnesota : Magic Wagon, 2019. | Series: Robyn Hood;
    book 1
Summary: Robyn and the Hoods must discover who is taking money from a local
    orphanage before the kids' fates are put in danger.
Identifiers: ISBN 9781532133763 (lib. bdg.) | ISBN 9781532134364 (ebook) | ISBN
    9781532134661 (Read-to-me ebook)
Subjects: LCSH: Stealing--Juvenile fiction. | Thieves--Juvenile fiction. |
    Orphanages--Juvenile fiction. | Adventure stories--Juvenile fiction.
Classification: DDC [FIC]--dc23

TABLE OF CONTENTS

Chapter One

METROPOLIS
ORPHANAGE

"Will you three stop

GOOFING off?" Robyn Hood

said to her friends Cole, Jasper,

and Silas. They were her loyal

SiDEKiCKS. Everyone

called them the Hoods.

"Whatever you say, boss,"

Cole replied.

The boys stopped *juggling* fruit and put it back on the stand. The fruit seller gave them a dirty look.

Metropolis Market was crowded like always. Robyn and the Hoods were supposed to be on the **LOOKOUT** for pickpockets.

Robyn felt a tap on her shoulder. She turned around and came face to chest with a tall, LANKY girl. She looked about the same age as Robyn.

"You're Robyn Hood, right?" the girl asked, **HUNCHING** over a bit. "The orphan who *STEALS* from bad guys to help people?"

"That's me," Robyn replied. "What's wrong?"

"Metropolis Orphanage is in **TROUBLE**," she explained.

"There is a **RUMOR** that the orphanage is running out of money, but no one knows why. The building is falling apart. Can you **HELP**?"

Robyn and the Hoods LOOKED at each other with concern. "Don't worry. We'll get to the bottom of . . ." Robyn started to say.

She turned back to face the girl, but she was already GONE.

Chapter Two
FAMILY
AFFAIR

"Any **leads**?" Robyn asked.
The Hoods were gathered
around a small, steel table. They
were on the first floor of the
ABANDONED
warehouse they had made their
home.

The Hoods had just returned from **LOOKING** for information about the orphanage.

Silas placed a BEAT-UP tablet on the table. "No one seems to know much, but I searched the government archives for OLD newspaper records. I came across this."

"Maybe someone is **STEALING** from the trust," Robyn said. "I'm going to the orphanage to see what I can find."

Soon, Robyn was creeping through Metropolis Orphanage to the director's office. She could see from the **SHABBY** halls and rooms that the girl hadn't been lying. The place was falling apart.

But no one was talking about what was going on at the orphanage. And to Robyn that could only mean one thing. Someone in **CHARGE** was behind this.

Robyn PICKED the lock and stepped inside. The office was pristine and sparse. She **strode** past framed degrees on the wall.

She stopped when she *noticed* the name on one certificate: Lois Dalton Fremont.

Chapter Three

WHAT GOES
AROUND . . .

"Why do we always have to **SCALE** buildings? None of you take my **FEAR** of heights seriously," Jasper whined.

They were climbing up the side of a *fancy* apartment building in the heart of Metropolis.

"**SHHHHH!**" Robyn chided. "It's that window on the right."

After leaving the orphanage earlier that day, Robyn and the Hoods SEARCHED more government archives. They confirmed that Lois Fremont was Bernard Dalton's daughter.

If anyone had **easy** access to the trust, it was her.

"We're in," Cole said,

LOOKING up from the tablet.

The Hoods' HACKING

skills came in handy for a lot

of things, especially disarming

security systems.

Robyn pushed open the window, and they climbed through. Inside was the most *lavish* apartment she had ever seen. Everything was plated in gold, and expensive-looking **JEWELRY** was out on display.

"Start collecting **JEWELRY** to use for ransom," Robyn instructed. "I'll look around to see what else I can find. We don't have much **TIME**. She could be getting home any minute."

Robyn headed into the director's bedroom. The *fancy* clothes in the walk-in closet caught her **EYE**, so she went in.

Robyn noticed something on the wall behind the clothes. "A **safe**," she breathed.

Robyn got to work trying to **crack** the code. Then Cole yelled, "We've got company!" Robyn heard the **BEEPS** of someone entering a code on the keypad outside the apartment door.

"FOCUS!" she told herself.

"Robyn, now!" Jasper cried as the **safe** popped open to reveal stacks of money.

"I bet this is trust money," Robyn whispered. She stuffed her backpack with the stacks.

In its place she left a note
that read *Docks, midnight. Alone.*
Then she DISAPPEARED
through the window.

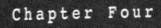

Chapter Four

. . . COMES
AROUND

"People **NEVER** follow directions," Cole sighed. Lois Fremont APPROACHED the dock. Two henchmen were with her.

"More fun for us," Jasper said.

The trio *FLEW* out of the shadows.

They took the director and henchmen by **SURPRISE**. The Hoods circled the henchmen with rope and pulled it tight. The henchmen fell forward head first. The **IMPACT** knocked them out.

The director **RAN** for a boat to hide on. But Robyn and the Hoods **JUMPED** on board just as she rounded the corner.

"Give. Me. My. Money.

And my **JEWELRY!**"

she shouted.

"We know you've been

STEALING from the trust," Robyn

said. "That money belongs to the

orphanage."

The director started **laughing**. "You . . . you're just kids!" She laughed even harder.

"We're thirteen!" Cole said **DEFIANTLY**. "Hardly children. And it doesn't matter anyway. The truth is the truth."

"You're right, kid," the director said to their SURPRISE. "And do you know what the **TRUTH** is? The **TRUTH** is that everyone. Is. An. Idiot. My stupid father. The stupid board of directors.

"So easily **FOOLED**! Why should my family's money be spent on good-for-nothing kids? I deserve that money, all of it! I only took what should have been mine."

Sirens **RANG** out in the distance.

"I guess stupid RUNS in the family," Robyn said.

She **HELD** up a cell phone. The authorities had been on the line for the director's confession.

The sirens **blared** louder. The Hoods tied up the director as Robyn placed the ransom bags next to her.

"You'll pay for this!" the director SHOUTED. She was taken away in handcuffs.

But for Robyn and the Hoods,

this was just another **DAY**,

another CRIME solved.